Skevington's Daughter

OLIVER REYNOLDS

Skevington's Daughter

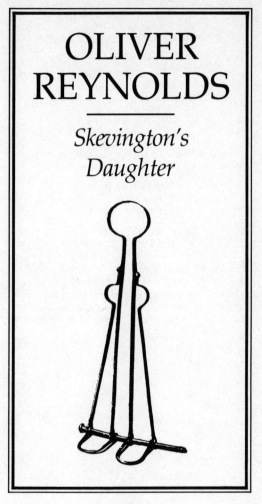

faber and faber

LONDON · BOSTON

First published in 1985
by Faber and Faber Limited
3 Queen Square London WC1N 3AU
Reprinted 1985

Filmset by Wilmaset, Birkenhead, Merseyside
Printed in Great Britain by
Redwood Burn Ltd, Trowbridge
All rights reserved

© Oliver Reynolds, 1985

British Library Cataloguing in Publication Data

Reynolds, Oliver
Skevington's daughter.
I. Title
821'.914   PR6068.E9/

ISBN 0–571–13697–4
ISBN 0–571–13546–3 Pbk

Contents

III

Acknowledgements

'Victoriana' first appeared in *Spectrum*.
The main events in this poem are described in
Caught in the Web of Words, the biography of Murray
by his granddaughter, K. M. Elisabeth Murray.

I

Victoriana

The up-train pulled into Crowthorne,
Grey smoke huddling from its funnel,
As Dr Murray finished *The Times*.
The Boers must capitulate soon.

Pistons blew off relieved hisses.
'Dead on,' murmured Dr Murray.
His watch snuck back to its pocket
Beneath the soft sweep of his beard.

(Its fringes were to ebb slightly
Later on, in 1904,
Following his brave ascent of
Le Pic de la Croix de Belledonne.

He said afterwards his beard froze
Into one huge blue icicle.
A plank was set under his chin
And the ice smashed out by hammer.)

Dr Murray was editing
A New English Dictionary
On Historical Principles.
(We know it as the *OED*.)

He was in Berkshire to visit
One of his main contributors,
Dr Minor, who often sent
Over a thousand quotes a month.

The annual Dictionary Dinner
Had long marked the passage of each
Lexicographical year.
Invitations went out to all.

Minor had declined every time
'Because of physical reasons'
(His elaborate calligraphy
Always scuttled across these words).

It was not until this year though
That Murray was asked to Crowthorne.
Train doors slammed on the platform
Like a sloppily drilled gun salute.

A man in livery came over.
'Dr Murray? Right. The sursiks.'
He picked up Murray's two cases
And nodded at a brougham outside.

Though an expert on dialect,
Murray still had his lacunae.
He unfastened a bound notebook
As the man flicked on the horses.

'A sursik, sir? It's a doodah.
Doofer. Thingummybob. Whatsit.
I first heard it from a Spaniard.
El Bunny, we called him. Buck teeth.'

After a journey of two miles
The brougham slewed into a courtyard.
Stray gravel on the wide flagstones
Snapped and spat beneath the wheel rims.

Murray pointed at some cracked stones.
'Steady on! If you don't slow down
All this will be crazy paving.'
'Just the place for it,' said the man.

Drawing up to the door, he leant
Over to yank on the bell-pull.
Seconds passed before distant sounds
Echoed, faint as lost memories.

*   *   *

Firelight wallowed in the shined wood
Of the escritoire. Murray coughed.
A small coal spun into the grate.
The clock heaved slow and heavy ticks.

He had been waiting ten minutes.
A servant had lit him along
Shadowed stairs and dark corridors
To this heavily curtained room.

After pouring Murray some tea
He had left 'to find the guv'nor'.
He had locked the door behind him.
Murray had sipped once from his cup.

'Dr Murray, you must forgive me.
I'm so sorry you had to wait.'
A man stood in the door, smiling.
Bunched keys slithered in his hands

And extravagant flossy tufts
Billowed from his ears like gunsmoke.
Murray rose and held out a hand.
'Dr Minor. Pleased to meet you.'

'Minor? No. I'm the Governor.
You should have been told long ago.
Bad form. This is the Broadmoor
Criminal Lunatic Asylum.'

* * *

They let Minor work on his own.
He had a study in East 4
And every week deliveries
Would arrive from the booksellers.

His room pullulated with words
As if it were the site of some
Gutenbergian breeding scheme.
Each flat surface was legible.

Minor sat in the windowseat,
His face ambushed by rearing clouds.
Murray's armchair bided its time,
A springy, book-propped booby-trap.

Skirting the unmentionable,
The conversation was awkward
And only grew easier when
They discussed Aristotle's death.

(Neither believing the theory
That he died of grief, unable
To discover the cause of
The ebb and flow of the Epirus.)

Rain fell as they neared the station.
Murray watched spray arc from the wheels.
On his lap was a small package.
The driver talked about Minor.

* * *

Minor was an American.
Serving with the Army of the North
As a surgeon-captain, he'd had
What was described as a bad war.

From the everyday charnel chores,
The cauters and amputations,
Only one memory remained:
The branding of a deserter.

(It had not taken him too long
To learn the Hippocratic oath,
Resting his Greek dictionary
On the balustrade's slick white

While he sunned himself on the porch.
That had been several years ago
And was all forgotten now as
He took the iron from the fire.)

Two lieutenants held the man down.
One, grunting, straddled his bare back.
Saliva coiled into the dust.
Heat-haze buzzed around the iron.

The audible crisping of flesh
And the sudden reek of shocked blood
Were as routine as mud or tents:
Old battlefield familiars.

What Minor did not expect, though,
Was for the man to look at him
With eyes awash with tears and sweat
Before he finally passed out.

That look was to stay with Minor.
A face sinking down through water;
The eyes, spilt blurs, emptying fast
Above a mute and stricken mouth.

Demobbed, he suffered from sunstroke
And persecution mania.
After spells in an asylum
He was pronounced well and released.

Then in 1871
Minor came over to England.
(A Professor at Yale gave him
An introduction to Ruskin.)

In the following year he had
His most persistent delusion:
He was pursued by Irishmen
Who'd sworn to revenge the branding.

Ovid's poems, in one pocket
Of Minor's winter overcoat,
Were now balanced by a pistol.
Fingers clawed on paper and steel.

Late on February 17th
He thought he was being followed.
The man he shot dead was, in fact,
The Lion Brewery's night stoker.

The down-train drew out of Crowthorne
As Murray's smug watch settled back.
Rolling smoke shrouded the windows.
Murray unwrapped Minor's present.

It was a copy of Ovid.
Riffling through it, he found pages
Dotted with globules of dried glue:
Braille tracks healing the torn paper.

Reading

Within the dark night, a house.
Within that, a room with one corner lit.
Within that, my head and a book.

And then this, the strangest recession:
I am there, but not there.
I am reading.

'It takes you out of yourself.'
Easy as taking a hand out of a pocket.
But hands don't float off.

Dark clamours at the window.
Moths batter the bulb.
I read on.

My body dwindles.
Thinned by text, it becomes Euclidean:
It has position but no magnitude.

An hour later, it returns;
Slowly, as if dropping by parachute.
I yawn and head for the toilet.

In bed, I pull up the blankets.
Night's tribunes call the room to order.
The moths stutter across the wall.

I have read too much.
Asleep, I read on.
Words and images dribble on to the pillow.

The left arm of Michelangelo's David
Was broken into three pieces by a bench
Hurled from the Palazzo Vecchio.

Restored, the arm now burns.
The white marble has a dark skin of smoke.
The hand waves through the flames.

Parisien

I work in the municipal glade.
Today I have to coax the cuckoo,
Sharing my bread with him,
Possibly soaking it in milk.
At least my tobacco is safe.

I am happiest when I leave,
Looping the chain
Like metal vine
Through the rusty gates
And clicking the lock.

I often pause then,
Hang my bag
(Holding a wine bottle and some crumbs)
On one of the railings
And take in the dusk.

Opposite the entrance,
Perched like flotsam above
The cobbled swell of the street,
Is a large wedge of apartments
Including my own.

In the half-light the building
Has a provisional look,
As if it were the memory of a film-still
Seen long ago outside a suburban cinema
Closed due to illness.

Faced by the Real Thing, the Critic Demurs

The cerulean was clearly mixed by the artist
And probably then applied by pupils,
But whoever impastoed the clouds
On today's massive sky
Was no apprentice.

All their perspectived billows are true;
All their shadows incontrovertible.
Their colours are
More than easy
On the eye.

The wind is immanent in the grass of the field
Which tilts away sharply from the viewer
To a bright distant green corner
Where a sunlit tree flourishes
Like an incomplete *fecit*.

At the front runs a river in fluxive sashays.
She was a forerunner of Capability's best,
But while he is long dead
Her waters still work,
Landskipping.

The whole composition is unified by
Breathed sunlight and golden air,
An omnilucent symbiosis
Visibly celebrating
Inseparability.

Straddling the stools of art and reality as it does,
One cannot conclude whether the work
Was drawn from life
Or created
In vacuo.

V & L

Vector licks us into shape.
Set-Square bellowing decrees
Rules out all hope of escape.

I, Rhombus, contemplate rape
Ogling Polygon's bent knees.
Vector licks us into shape.

Dodecahedron wears crêpe.
His cosine's sudden decease
Rules out all hope of escape.

Letters lay claim to inscape.
V counts L's ninety degrees.
Vector licks us into shape.

Pi offers Lozenge a grape.
Her sly eagerness to please
Rules out all hope of escape.

'Just love this linear jape!'
Euclid, the local big cheese,
Rules out all hope of escape.
Vector licks us into shape.

Cold War

Their motor oil froze.
Our best defence against
Panzers and half-tracks
Was snow and the cold.
They were 80 kilometres from Moscow.
Once again we had traded land for time.
It had beaten Napoleon.
Now it was being tried with Hitler.

The first slush had bogged them down.
Put in charge of Moscow,
Zhukov organized tank traps.
Everyone dug.
The slush solidified and they moved up.
Their guns could be heard from the suburbs.
(In Berlin, women made parcels of furs
For their boys on the Russian front.)

Up until then it had been a doddle.
They had rolled through cornfields,
Their sights filling with easy prey
(We lost 6,000 tanks in two engagements).
At breakfast, the crews would look east:
The faint line was either the horizon
Or sight petering out.
Our old equation: land swapped for time.

They made jokes about
The earth being flat after all.
We sent for troops from Siberia.
They grumbled about their footwear
And watched compass needles
Swing and falter
As if confused by the flatness.
Then their motor oil froze.

* * *

Meyer was captured early on.
I had to interrogate him.
What little hard intelligence he had
Came out in the first hour.
He had no idea of battle plans
And was vaguely aware that Moscow
'Was the big town in the distance'.
He explained the genitive case to me.

We spent the last session
Talking about books and women,
But without interrupting the war.
Pushkin was blitzed by Goethe;
Tolstoy pounded Schiller.
All Russian women were peasants;
All Germans frigid.
He had a hiccupy laugh.

The day after, he was the signpost.
Hauling a sled, he slipped and fell.
A T34, not bothering to swerve,
Pulped his trunk to winter mulch.
His legs skeetered to the roadside
Where a lorry was to clip the feet,
Squishing them into the snow.
The legs levered into the air.

They had soon frozen
And were used as a marker
For the turn-off to the stores.
We left them when we advanced
And they probably still stand,
A Teutonic Ozymandias
Surrounded by snow
Or sunk under blizzards.

Acholba

There were ten nouns
For the different
States of sand.
Two verbs described
Its crunch when eaten.

Bad luck was always
As welcome as
A sandy foreskin.
Our Sisyphus
Counted grains.

It was an oral culture.
Nothing was fixed.
The past was fluid
And it changed
With each telling.

The stories confused me.
When I tried to count
The number of men
Claiming to be my father,
I ran out of fingers.

Missionaries taught us
To read and write
In their language.
The youngsters
Learned quickly.

Not the elders, though:
They distrusted a world
Where the past
Had been tidied
Into immobility.

Some feared that
The new tongue
Would kill the old.
One decided to fast,
Silent in the desert.

He visited me
Before he left.
I had to show him
How to write the name
Of the old language.

He would use it
To fill the desert,
A charm written
Over and over
In the sand.

Reminiscence

They buried Pinchbeck in St Dunstan's.
That's in Fleet Street
Not far from his old workshop
(Under the sign of the Astronomico-Musical clock)
And within pissing distance of the Leg Tavern.

Last time I saw him was in the Leg.
Both of us ratted.
The hangovers he must have had.
Amazes me how he ever got up,
Never mind finicking with those watches.

He showed me the case for his latest.
All of it pinchbeck, of course,
With a funny spike-like affair at the top.
'The acme of innovatory chronometry.'
Try saying that when you're cut.

This spike opened and closed
Just like a beak.
The whole thing was to be for George II.
Pinchbeck called it
His royal mocking-watch.

It whistled the quarters
And chirruped the hours.
The striking-mechanism was just that.
Pinchbeck had devised a complex damper
For evening use.

He was especially proud
Of the watch's sensitivity:
It fell silent
Whenever covered
With an opaque cloth.

He had got the idea
When feeding his pet songbird.
This had been caught long before
And was now kept in a cage in the workshop.
It had been trained to tell the time.

Every hour on the hour,
Regular as clockwork,
It would pipe out the required number
Of clear double-notes
(A little like those of the cuckoo).

Once when Pinchbeck was still in bed
I examined the bird as it sang noon.
It had knowledgeable eyes
And a pert head
Which it turned stiffly with each note.

I'm not sure now,
But after the twelve measured calls
And before the normal song was resumed
There seemed to be
A snickering of ratchets.

Pastoral

For E. Delacroix, Nature is
a vast dictionary.
Baudelaire

Here, overhung with estovers,
The brook is aquiver with quim.
After tittupping his plovers,
The Heaviside Layer looks grim.

Rain keeps falling, as if sorry.
Thunder madronoes, echoing
Falls off the back of a lorry.
Beyond the hill, zuz softly sing.

An eth slowly sways to its byre.
Tardigrade clouds parse to the west.
Gordian lightning strikes a spire.
Heaviside is soaked and depressed.

I cast deftly over the brook,
Juicy lammies weighting my hook.

E. Delacroix, Pleinairist

An ox lows, Old High German
Bordering on Late Latin.
Clouds pursue their
Diverse etymologies.
Each shower of rain
Falls in italics.
Geese cross the sky,
Heading for Appendix II.
I wait in the supplement,
Jostled by the entry on sheep.

Anna Colutha in Suffolk

I first saw her in a teashop in Eye.
We had both been stood up
And it showed.
She kept looking at her watch
As if it was to blame.
I marshalled a smile
Then crossed to her table.
We had a pot for two
And drank to absent shits.
The hatchback is easier to load.

She was an astronomer
Working on black holes.
If sucked into one head first
The greater pull on the upper body
Results in stretching of the trunk.
This is known as spaghettification.
She spoke quickly,
Holding up a glass as the black hole
And circling it with one very white hand.
Boycott had just made his hundredth hundred.

I was working my way up to Diss.
At each stop
I puzzled over
Araucaria's latest
Until all but 10 Down were done.
Anna had it straight away,
Filling it in with her propelling pencil.
(It was 'jerboa' which I later learned
Is also known as *Jaculus jaculus*.)
In Walberswick I went to the dentist's.

Random passion is rather confusing;
After I had dropped her off
I missed the turning for the A140.
Anna was very taken with my stomach
And used it as a pillow.
Moles ran in the Colutha family
And she had a beauty on her back,
Stuck there like a squashed sultana
Against the skin's eidetic white.
Bulk orders are on the up.

And

Some people are too old to listen.
One, green-fingered, has turned over
The seasons like four slow pages.
He now grafts to his plotted day,
Pushing canes into the earth
For his beans and peas
And finds the joints of his fingers
Mocked by those of the bamboo.

Some are too young to understand.
Until now harm has been domestic
Or waiting in the stream or road
(And never take sweets from strangers).
The ABC included fire
And cuts and tears
But not this searing sky
And the toy train melted on its tracks.

Some don't believe it.
Monks on an island retreat
Look heavenward for a sign
And then kneel helpless.
Light crackles above a furrowing sea.
Water froths and bubbles
As if some god blew invisible straws
Into the emptying glass of the world.

Some cannot be told.
Dolphins butt the troughs,
Sonar jamming as the sea silts.
One slews dead-weight to the bottom,
An embryo jerking her belly.
Elephants remembering scream for Noah.
Birds fly into nothing.
Their songs fall as dust.

II

Album

(From the Latin
Albus, white.)

This baby on the lawn will soon
Fade altogether.

The sunstruck grass already
Bleeds albescent.

Weak chemicals give up their ghosts.
Swirls of shadow falter.

Only the white of the smock holds,
Sucking from the photo's centre.

It fixes on the eye-hole of the sun,
Punched through the sky.

It drains the once-pink arms,
Absorbs the face.

The dark mouth will be the last to go
As all turns to tundra.

Picture and borders
Are one.

[41]

Watching the Birdie

And us caught
Smiling.

Facing up
To unhappiness,

We hold hands
As if glued.

The shutter falls,
A tiny axe.

Cheese!

And that's me with the moustache
(Newcombe out of Zapata)
And the eyes consigned
To middle distance.
Each arm drapes shoulders
(Dave's and Leonard's).
One leg folds protectively
In front of the other.

Under the right arm, Julie,
As if sprung from a rib.
She and I, doused in the doorstep's sun,
Coffee still sliding in the stomach,
Both caught by the morning
After the night before.
She and I yet to know how distant
That past will look from this future.

Our first time,
Stars crowding the small window,
Was drunk and fumbling
But also light-hearted:
Our flesh enjoyed its blunders.
Hostages to fortune,
We laughed
And snuggled into our bonds.

Shortly before dawn, Leonard,
Product of an English Public School,
Entered the room and woke us
By pissing in a corner.
He did this at other parties that term
Without recalling a thing the next day.
It seemed a novel
Extension of sleepwalking.

The duvet absorbed
Third-party damage.
In the morning I found my shoes
Were one shade lighter.
A hardback Auden was still sopping.
I stood it up in the grate
Where its covers
Dried into parentheses.

I was taking a degree
At the university down the road,
But got more from tutorials
On that mattress on the floor.
History was previous lovers.
Geography was tactile.
We both got distinctions
In Practical Biology.

A Canadian once compared
Julie's eyes to fried eggs.
A Pole christened her breasts
Winston and Saunders
(Winston was dextral,
Saunders sinister).
I was Welsh
And got her pregnant.

[44]

As Julie described the abortion
She smoked three cigarettes.
She had used the new duvet
To swaddle herself
Like a papoose.
This was long after
That first night.
I think I had a beard by then.

Little Ease

Lubricious brass winks at iron.
Julie stands by the daughter,
A grin ripping her mouth
And her eyes red-balled
In the flash.

Skevington devised his machine
When Lieutenant of the Tower.
It compressed and doubled
The victim's body,
Forcing the head to the feet.

Nose and ears jerked blood,
Sometimes fingers and toes.
The machine was named
Skevington's Daughter
Or Little Ease.

Julie posed there some seconds:
Seconds passing as seconds
Then her grin and the flash
Both leaping
The huge dumb flags of the floor.

Back

The 'wick' of 'Walberswick'
Had been torn off.
Above the tear, fading,
The single word 'Mother'.
'That's Emmie's writing,'
Said my mother, as if
Recognizing a face,
Her memory instinct with
The slanted loop of letters
Long since read and lost.

The photo, a two-inch circle
Set in a black wood roundel,
Hung on the bedroom wall.
Behind the greening glass,
The head and shoulders
Of a woman in stiff black,
The long hair pinned up;
A small monkey-like face
And a grim slight smile
Rigid for the 1890 camera.

'Who's that?' I had asked.
'My grandmother. She lived
In Walberswick for a while.
She had four daughters.'
(These were Mabel, Emmie, Elsie
And Violet, my mother's mother.)
'I forget what she was called.'
So she turned the photo over
To find the torn place-name
And that single looped word.

[47]

Family Tree in Black and White

The room blanched
With each flash of magnesium.
(Thor would have been handy
In a photographic studio.)
White smoke bulged then thinned
To the high ceiling,
Paying wispful homage to Vesuvius.

Violet and Elsie, Emmie and Mabel
Breathed out, adjusted pince-nez,
Double-checked that their lockets
Lay flat
On bosom-stretched bombazine
Before freezing for the next one.
George shot his cuffs.

Years later, Violet, Elsie and Emmie
Rigidly hold their final pose.
Unseen leaves drift over them
As the feet of strangers
Criss-cross the sifting gravel.
Mabel smiles in her nursing home.
Aping the shutter, her dentures click.

She and her sisters (the Oliver girls)
Once ran a greengrocer's in Bournemouth.
Cousin George started
An antiques business in Southwold.
Past seventy, he is still the swell,
His pert red dicky-bow shushing
Any hints of grog-blossom.

Uncle Stan pours out lemonade
In the back-garden of 'Rosewood'.
(He and mother grew up here
With Great Aunt Mabel and Gomer
Whose real wife was in an asylum.)
At the mouth of the bottle
A hinged wire clasp holds the stopper.

Beneath a sign reading 'High Street',
My father cradles a wrapped loaf.
A car chugs by, heading for
The vanishing point and Beaulieu.
Will I look like this at forty-plus:
Neat thin breadwinner, clear eyes
Above an assertive Adam's apple?

The last son makes his entrance.
Aged four, he grimly points
A toy sword at the yawning sky.
Abrupt scissors have ruled his fringe.
There must be others of him,
Lost amongst the negatives
And left undeveloped.

Stills

Blake, four, helps Dorothy in the garden.
She smiles down at the wet earth.
Leaves brush the skin
On the inside of her arm.
Her son holds an aluminium teapot
By its black Bakelite handle.
Pure narrow twists arc from the spout
To the slopping puddle beneath.
The braces, clutching his shorts,
Are on back to front.

An ocean away
(They married and emigrated in '51)
The big sky is like a promise kept.
Cousin Russell swims in sun.
(We will meet as confused boys,
Cardiff and Montreal
Already stamped on our accents.)
Stanley, his father, pours sand
From cupped fist to flat palm.
Each grain has its place in the air.

Violet and Emlyn rest hands
On their children's shoulders.
Dorothy and Stanley
Smile into the wind.
The Dunster sky huddles above them.
Though hair flickers into faces
And a skirt swings like a bell,
Emlyn's hat is as steady as a rock.
The sea's fretwork
Lapses at their feet.

Smile, Please

Track it through the pages
Back to its first appearance

Some time after her parents died
Within months of each other

When she was
Still only sixteen.

That's when it stopped
Having anything to do with happiness

And started being something
Laid on top of her face.

That's when it started
Being conscious.

That smile was there to be recorded,
As neutral as her clothes

Or the shine of her brother's hair-oil
(Next to her in the garden at 'Rosewood').

She smiled formally, in the way
An old man might tip his hat.

Each decade tightened it
Into the rigor of the living,

But occasionally there was
A second's pleasure,

A hint of a suburban Gioconda
Framed by the rockery

And the 2.10 from Coryton
Rattling by in the background.

Orwell said we all at fifty
Have the face we deserve.

Some of us though
Disclaim responsibility,

Ducking the sentence for a moment
As stretched lips plead our innocence.

Smiles lodge our appeal
Before we return to the face's lock-up.

But not hers.
Her smile is a frown on bail,

The mouth led astray
By the hunched brow.

Camera Lucida

Her arm bent. The thin young elbow.
A poised and balletic fleetness.
The bathing-cap tight on her round head.
Next to her, ample and smiling, her mother.
Sky meeting Dunster Beach: another snug fit.
Scrawls of foam puff across the shingle.
The flat sea stretches
Then bumps up into Welsh hills.
Her mother's face is rounded, spectacled;
The short simple hair untouched by the wind.
Violet Jones. The daughter has yet to link
The name to the mother's easy bulk.
One arm high, she skips beside her as if
Sprung from that old smile on to spellbound sand.

Camera Obscura

Emlyn took the photo in '25,
The year he painted the chalet's name-plate:
'PARADISE REGAINED. No Hawkers.'
(Later, back at his desk at the GWR,
He would reverse his trouser turn-ups
And watch paint-clogged sand strew the lino.)
Violet and Dorothy shrieked at the lens,
The girl's arm wriggling like a fish.
The tripod rose from a welter of footprints,
Small toes squidging into his heel marks.
Castles had been razed by noughts and crosses.
He hitched his braces and focused.
The sky shrunk in the viewfinder.
The sullen sea sloped off into nothing.

Dissolve

Born in Walbers,
I arrived amidst
The repeated *thok*!
Of flashlight bulbs
With a neat centre parting.

Mother found it
An easy delivery:
'Like shelling peas.'
My bright basso cries
Were in tripping sol-fa.

At four, I trebled
The family fortune
(Based on antiques and
The Dunster sepia mines)
By cunning disinvestment.

Due to
My nurse
(38–26–32),
My upbringing
Was comprehensive.

She let me
Play in the attic
So long as I never
Opened the cupboard
Built out into the eaves.

Of course
I disobeyed;
Our skeleton
Was adjusting
A pert red dicky-bow.

Blushing,
I ran back to nurse
Who took my injured pride
And slowly kissed it better.
My childhood was thus soon over.

Experienced
But gullible,
I was married young
To Skevington's daughter
And barely escaped the wedding-night.

Luckily,
I was able
By a knack of the wrist
Learned from my Uncle Stan
To dispatch her to the eaves.

My second marriage
Continues to hold good.
I write this warm in bed
In a Bournemouth penthouse
Resting the paper on my wife's back.

Haiga
Sprawls my lap
And reads Goethe,
Beating out the metres
The length of my tensed thighs.

Phutts!
Nudge the window
As her grandfather
Mows the lawn far below,
Unswathing the long afternoon.

An unorthodox Jew,
He wears his yarmulka
Only when sat on the mower:
The dark cap bobbling through
The bitty bow-waves of sliced green.

This then
Is how things are:
My happiness settling
Like a smile being fixed
As it swims up through developer.

Rounding off such a well-composed life,
The final snaps should be perfect.
No doubt I'll make
A photogenic
Corpse.

Self-Portrait

You need regular brushing
Of the whites of your eyes.

(Pecker is maintained
By talking to oneself
In assumed voices.)
I have a beard now.
I stand against a window.

Stomach in, chest out.
No more pocket billiards.

Next to the back of my head,
Reflected in the top pane,
A squat shadow
Lifts a small box to its face.
A stranger at the feast.

Watch the birdie, darlings.
Eyes and teeth, eyes and teeth.

I squint into sunlight,
Afraid of posterity
Holding me responsible
For the way I look.
I look askance.

No take click-picture me.
Him kill my spirit.

Lop-sided truculence,
I am the Hunchback
Of Rhiwbina Garden Village.
The shadow in the window
Crooks its finger.

Crops

Father is only visible below the waist.
His trouser-legs sag as if deflated.
The shoes though shine solidly.

Two of the Oliver sisters hold hands.
(They gave me my first name.)
Their heads are missing.

Half of Violet dabbles with the sea.
Priming tides renew and falter
Like Cheyne-Stokes breathing.

My arm is sliced off by a margin
And disappears with whatever
It was doing or holding.

The reaper eyes us, gauging the distance.
He is putting off the hard choice
Between Instamatic and scythe.

III

Dysgu

After two months in earphones
We can cope with the mundane
So long as it's slow.
But we're in mined territory:
'Are you near- or far-sighted?'
'I live five minutes away.'

In the coffee-break
Maxwell Sirenya
Reads the overseas news.
An exile from South Africa,
He speaks Welsh
With a Xhosan accent.

Newland, the oldest, remembers
Cycling home alongside
The Glamorganshire Canal
When it was still a canal:
A cone of light moving into dark
And the regular plop of frogs.

Each has his reason to be here
Speaking through declenched teeth:
I'd thought it time to stop
Welshing on the language
And learn about roots,
If only etymological ones.

Daearyddiaeth

The land was always worked.
It was what you lived on.
So the feelings were strong:
The land was in your heart;
The land was underfoot.

It's still farmed, flat and hill,
Some of it good, some bad.
Cash crops may oust *hiraeth*,
But it's still praised: *Gwlad, gwlad*
With the ball hanging air.

And many of the poems
Carry the smack of loam,
In books of earthy style
Whose pages you leaf through
Like someone turning soil.

It wasn't long before
Love and the land were one.
Sweethearts had their contours
While streams grew feminine.
Desire and greening joined.

The genre pullulated.
Venus came on vernal.
The body pastoral
Was sung or lamented
As was Arthur's, grass-graved.

What though of city loves?
Hamlet's country matters
Aren't foreign to the town:
We've enough to ensure
Cupid stays urban.

Poets of the precincts
Lacking parallels
Instinct with the instincts
Should exchange Arcady
For the brick of Cardiff.

Fingers that divagate
Along the vertebrae
Assume Sanquahar Street,
Sesquipedalian
Way to the timber yards.

The gasworks surplus burns
Behind Jonkers Terrace.
Wind flutes and twists the flame,
The gold column broken
Into plaits and tresses.

The path to Thornbury Close
Dwindles into Thornhill
Where tight dawn is seeping
Bit by bit into day:
Someone slowly waking.

At the side of the path
Is an old lamp-standard
Whose bulb is lit but pale
Above the base's stamped
And simple avowal:

D. Evans   Eagle Foundry
Llandaff   1911.

Asgwrn Cefn y Beic

A while now since he dismounted.
Foraging, his fingers assess
The length of her still-tacky spine.

She is leaning against the wall,
Absorbed in *The Third Policeman*.
One of his knees nudges her seat.

Giving in taut waves, folded flesh
Hummocks above the knuckling bones'
Smoothed and stubborn crenellation.

Castling, he skims the long hollow.
Mated, grinning, she shuts the book.
His fingers, Marcher Lords, push south.

Poeth ac Oer

Season of small gains
In a land of small victories.
Flakes lag the sky
And tortoises hibernate,
Their hearts slowed
To eleven beats a minute;
Eleven tentative beats
Ticking into March.

A writer gauges her face
In the bathroom mirror.
She leans on the taps
Which dribble solid water
Then goes back to the study
With stamped palms:
Reversed P on the one hand,
O on the other.

Pancake day.
Clouds stumble over hills
And then thin.
Snow, after filling bowls
Left outside kitchen doors,
Is sifted into batter.
Small hearts lurch
Into twelve beats a minute.

Awen I

Gold makes a woman penny-white.
So they say.

(Or did – before penny-white
Got its *obs*. in the *OED*.)

Meaning the old bint's
Only worth it if she's loaded.

So is that the form then
On you and this Poetry piece?

I mean either she's stinking
Or you're beswick.

Otherwise
Why knock round with her?

Awen II

It has to be feminine.
First the old afflatus
Busy in the Fallopians.

Then the writing thing.
Sitting down
For your verbal D and C.

And then finally this:
The scrapings
Ready for analysis.

Ch

In their own alphabet
This is fourth,
A train in labour
Stalled at the mouth
Of the throat's tunnel.

Fetishists relish
Bits of the body,
Hair tressed or plaited;
Why not go for the heard
And dote on vocables?

Unlike China's bound feet,
This constriction
Is self-inflicted.
The palate tightens
Over the consonant.

Chwap, for instance,
Takes you from the start.
Lifted swooning, dammed up,
Your only release
Is the coming vowel.

Gwroniaid

Lapping renown,
They run from us:
Guto Nyth Brân
And Zola Budd.

Guto sprints,
Leaving death stitched.
The chested tape
Trails down decades.

She runs barefoot
At Stellenbosch.
Afrikaners
Clap rhythmically.

Do they follow
Her double-beat
Or do her feet
Follow their hands?

Thin and frowning,
She prints spondees
Along the track:
J'accuse. J'accuse.

They modulate
And then quicken
To beat jagged:
Xhosa. Xhosa.

Halen

*Defnydd o ddŵr y môr, etc., ac a
ddefnyddir i roi blas ar fwydydd.*

We've returned again to childhood
Where teacher has answers off pat,
Where bad's always opposed by good
And hot by cold and dog by cat.

Pent now within these four walls,
The world deflates to blackboard size.
Shrunk to neat opposites, it falls
Prey to white chalk and whiter lies.

That way we avoid Babel II.
Facts irk when you're learning to speak:
Only say what you're able to,
Let's leave truth to a later week.

It's too early to talk of shades,
Of hues in-between or part-dyed.
Don't get into morals or grades;
Talk of the rain, not apartheid.

Truth waits on vocabulary.
Words keep thoughts in proper places,
Grammatic constabulary
Patrolling all open spaces.

Our world is simple, simply viewed,
And the simplest of all is salt.
Sea-given, it seasons our food,
Its simpleness proof against fault.

[73]

We've no need to know of cellars,
Who sits above, who sits below;
And we want no one to tell us
Of wounds being rubbed till they glow.

That sea gives salt and salt savour
Is truth enough for all our years.
And should tears have any flavour,
It isn't of salt, but of tears.

Amheuaeth

The walls curve here,
Smooth and cool to the touch,
Then taper above our closed eyes.

We lean back on them,
High and secure
In this high cool pinnacle.

Others far below
Clack
Through the gates of horn.

We ignore them,
Having pulled up behind us
The ladder of our language.

We shape ourselves
To these cool walls
And dream ivory dreams.

Ifori

Yes – building material
For high-rise ideology,
But not only that.

Protean, it reminds us
That objects, like languages,
Have their different uses.

In the raw, tusked,
It can ram or pierce.
Powdered, it is aphrodisiac.

It smiles evenly from pianos
And, round, kisses and cushions
Across pool tables.

The choice is ours – as with language:
We opt for retreat or ambush,
Aiming to snooker or impale.

Bechgyn Bando Margam, 1800–1859

They wore red and white
Like others later.
Their heyday was decades long
And is now forgotten.

The ball was shaped from wood,
The clasp-knife whittling
As they marked out the pitch
On common land or seashore.

We imagine snatches of Arcady
Won from shifts at pit or furnace:
The people playing on common land
Or framed by sea and watched by gulls.

They will have made their own sticks,
Lopped trees and scattered leaves
Marking the way of some thirty men
Set free on the heights of summer.

Pitching the posts with the other team,
They will have stood out clearly
Under the sky's primary blue
In their red and white.

Maes Chwarae

What is there in this air,
Once seeming so general
And omni-directional,
That now implodes it
To this one hanging point?

Seventy thousand heads
Gauge the parabola.
Seventy thousand hearts
Distend the chocked pause
Between one beat and the next.

Sunlight splits tiered concrete
And flares from face to face,
Coronal and unseen,
Then pans over grass
Chivvying chlorophyll.

Log-jammed about one spot,
Foci narrow and pack.
Their object hesitates.
High above, white cloud-bank
Balloons across the sun.

The ball drops, ovalling.
The posts point to the sky,
The crossbar between them
Neutral and dead-level
Like a line in a ledger.

Pobl y Cwm

Rhondda sounds hollow now,
A throne-room grown musty.
We've no news of King Coal
And the latest Mrs Simpson.

We fossick through slurry
And our thin sodden days:
Life on the canal bed
After the plug's been pulled.

Cantilever principles,
Proved with pit-prop
To secure lives,
Now find new uses.

They're expanding
The factory at Merthyr
That makes Janet Reger
Luxury Lingerie.

Anthracite is reclaimed
By the dictionary.
We read our future
In the bottom of a D-cup.

Thus my fingers fighting Gordius
Behind your back and up your blouse
Busy themselves with nothing less
Than the plight of Welsh Industry.

Athronydd yn Y Rhyl

Oxidizing unamused
Over four decades,
Victoria's profile
Deepened towards black.

Putting it in the slot,
The man wondered
Which of the two it was,
Cupreous or cupric?

It took a long time
For the penny to drop.
Der Groschen ist gefallen.
The shutter clicked open.

On the promenade
A boy with coppery hair
Was buying ice-cream.
Sand gritted his calves.

Pressed to the eyepiece,
The man reached out
As if to carefully
Brush off the sand.

Five hundred yards away
The boy paid,
One coin catching the sun.
Cupreous or cupric?

Telesgôp

*Offeryn i edrych trwyddo fel bod
chi'n gweld y pell yn agos.*

They sat together
In the Floral Hall's
Fusion of light,
Air, sun and glass.

One hour to walk
The prom's three miles.
The boy's calves ached.
You should rub them.

The man liked whistling.
He'd said his brother,
Though one-armed,
Was a concert pianist.

The panes above them
Had just been polished.
The two of them sat,
Drenched in sky.

The man wanted the boy
To teach him some Welsh.
*Sut basech chi'n
Diffinio telesgôp?*

They discussed books.
The man knew Housman.
*Odd chap. Forbade me
Use of his toilet.*

The boy was embarrassed.
He looked away,
Then out and up
Into the static sky.

Held by the blue,
He heard little
Of proposition
5.633.

Nothing that you see
In the visual field
Allows you to infer
It is seen by an eye.

A gull slid past,
Bleached and distinct,
With wings braced
As if carrying buckets.

The man said it was rare
For either seeing
Or consciousness
To be aware of itself.

When this happened though,
We approached reality.
As others use telescopes,
He'd like to use language.

The boy nodded, happy.
Far above the glass
The gull feathered,
Boosting on blue air.

[82]

Nodiad

DJs in Broadcasting House
Having trouble reading out
Birthday cards from Machynlleth,
Should note that the consonants
Ll and *ch* in Welsh resemble
Xl and *r* in Xhosa.

Cefn Gwlad

Always like this:
The standing field,
The climbing cloud.
And between them,
Lashed or drifted,
The falling rain;
Nothing to do
But fall and fall.

The image fixed
Many years back:
Land, sky and rain.
In addition,
The men at work
On the humped hill;
Then with horses,
Now with tractors.

Always like this:
The trust in soil
And long slow work
With rain sealing
The unnoticed
Blurred horizons;
The standing field,
The climbing cloud.

Dimai

How many years for half penny
To contract into ha'penny?
Probably no longer
Than the time it'll take
For most of us to forget both.

According to its detractors
It was used less and less;
Devalued by larger forces,
It was only retained
Through nostalgia.

Others accounted differently:
Those who kept it current
Found it burnished through use,
Each small exchange
Demonstrating its worth.

There was a daily assaying
In the home and at work:
They feared attempts
To counterfeit
Its exactitude and stability.

Now, disregarding other coinages,
They pass it on between themselves.
The hoard is made public.
There's no surprise
At its growing brighter with age.

Notes

83 *Nodiad*: note.
84 *Cefn Gwlad*: countryside.
85 *Dimai*: halfpenny.